WHAT HAPPENED TO AMELIA EARHART?

Other Baffling Mysteries in
A HISTORY MYSTERY *Series*
from Avon Camelot

THE CURSE OF THE HOPE DIAMOND
by Janet Hubbard-Brown

THE CURSE OF KING TUT'S TOMB
by Jay Montavon

THE DISAPPEARANCE OF THE ANASAZI
by Janet Hubbard-Brown

THE MYSTERY OF THE ROSWELL UFO
by Ken McMurtry

THE SECRET OF ROANOKE ISLAND
by Janet Hubbard-Brown

WHO SHOT JFK?
by Susan Landsman

Avon Books are available at special quantity discounts for bulk purchases for sales promotions, premiums, fund raising or educational use. Special books, or book excerpts, can also be created to fit specific needs.

For details write or telephone the office of the Director of Special Markets, Avon Books, Dept. FP, 1350 Avenue of the Americas, New York, New York 10019, 1-800-238-0658.

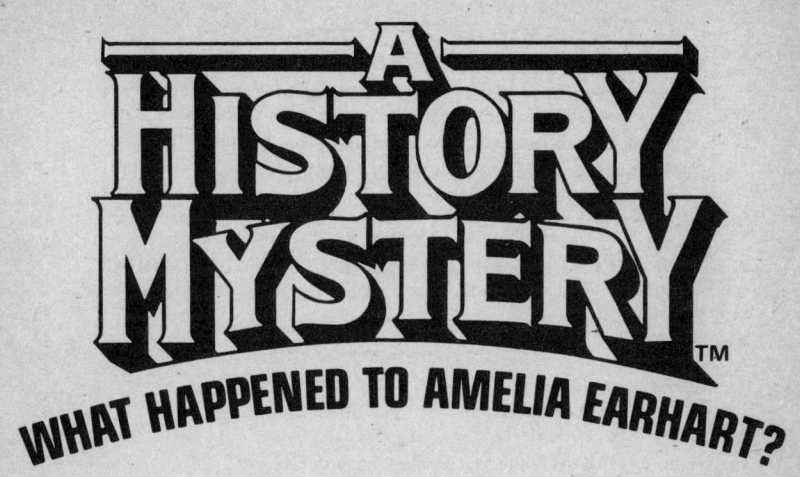

WHAT HAPPENED TO AMELIA EARHART?

SUSAN LANDSMAN

AN AVON CAMELOT BOOK

If you purchased this book without a cover, you should be aware that this book is stolen property. It was reported as "unsold and destroyed" to the publisher, and neither the author nor the publisher has received any payment for this "stripped book."

A HISTORY MYSTERY: WHAT HAPPENED TO AMELIA EARHART? is an original publication of Avon Books. This work has never before appeared in book form.

AVON BOOKS
A division of
The Hearst Corporation
1350 Avenue of the Americas
New York, New York 10019

Copyright © 1991 by Whitbread Books/Shannon Gilligan
Cover photograph courtesy FPG International
Maps by Bonnie Atwater
Published by arrangement with Whitbread Books
A History Mystery is a trademarked property of Shannon Gilligan/Whitbread Books.
Library of Congress Catalog Card Number: 91-6980
ISBN: 0-380-76221-8
RL: 5.9

All rights reserved, which includes the right to reproduce this book or portions thereof in any form whatsoever except as provided by the U.S. Copyright Law. For information address Whitbread Books, Fiddler's Green, Box 1, Waitsfield, Vermont 05673.

Library of Congress Cataloging in Publication Data:
Landsman, Susan.
    What happened to Amelia Earhart? / Susan Landsman.
        p. cm.—(A History Mystery) (An Avon Camelot book)
    Includes bibliographical references.
    Summary: Discusses the life of the famous aviator, including her childhood, flying records, and mysterious disappearance.
    1. Earhart, Amelia, 1897–1937—Juvenile literature. 2. Air pilots—United States—Biography—Juvenile literature.
[1. Earhart, Amelia, 1897–1937. 2. Air pilots.] I. Title. II. Series.
TL540.E3L36 1991   91-6980
629.13'092—dc20   CIP
[B]   AC

First Avon Camelot Printing: July 1991

CAMELOT TRADEMARK REG. U.S. PAT. OFF. AND IN OTHER COUNTRIES, MARCA REGISTRADA, HECHO EN U.S.A.

Printed in the U.S.A.
OPM   10 9 8 7 6 5 4 3

Table of Contents

Chronology	vii
Mayday!	1
First Flight	13
Across the Atlantic	25
Floating on Air	33
Around the World	43
Vanished!	59
What Happened to Amelia Earhart?	71
Bibliography	81

Chronology

1492—Leonardo da Vinci, the Italian artist and inventor, draws a "flying machine." It looks remarkably like a modern-day helicopter.

1670—Another Italian, scientist Giovanni Borelli, tries to use artificial wings to fly.

1897—On July 24, Amelia Otis Earhart is born in Atchison, Kansas.

1903—The Wright brothers of Ohio successfully fly an airplane. The first flight lasts eight seconds.

1908—Wilbur Wright flies 30 miles in 40 minutes.

WHAT HAPPENED TO AMELIA EARHART?

1909—Louis Bleriot crosses the English Channel from France to England. It takes him 37 minutes.

1914—World War I begins. It is the first war that will use flying machines.

1918—Amelia Earhart first comes into contact with flying while working as a nurse's aide in Toronto, Canada.

1918—The first regular airmail postage route is established between New York and Washington, D.C.

1922—Amelia buys her first plane. She calls it the *Canary* because of its yellow color.

1927—Charles Lindbergh flies the *Spirit of St. Louis* nonstop from New York to Paris, becoming the first human to cross a major ocean by plane.

CHRONOLOGY

1928—Amelia Earhart becomes the first woman to cross the Atlantic by plane aboard the *Friendship*. She flies as navigator, not pilot.

1929—The stock market crashes. The Depression begins and the roaring '20s come to an end.

1932—Amelia Earhart becomes the first woman to fly solo across the Atlantic. She flies from Newfoundland to Londonderry, Ireland, in 13.5 hours.

1937—Amelia Earhart disappears over the Pacific Ocean in her quest to become the first person to fly around the earth.

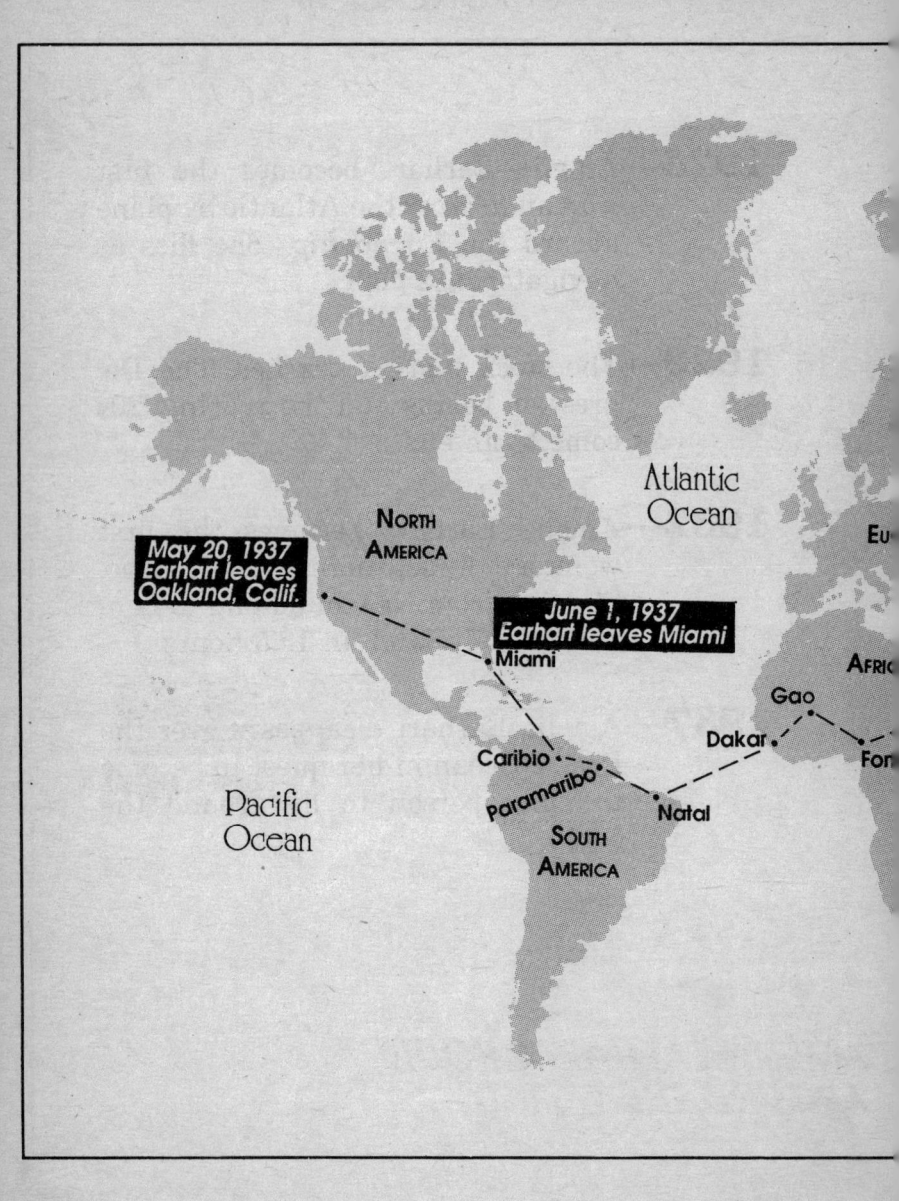

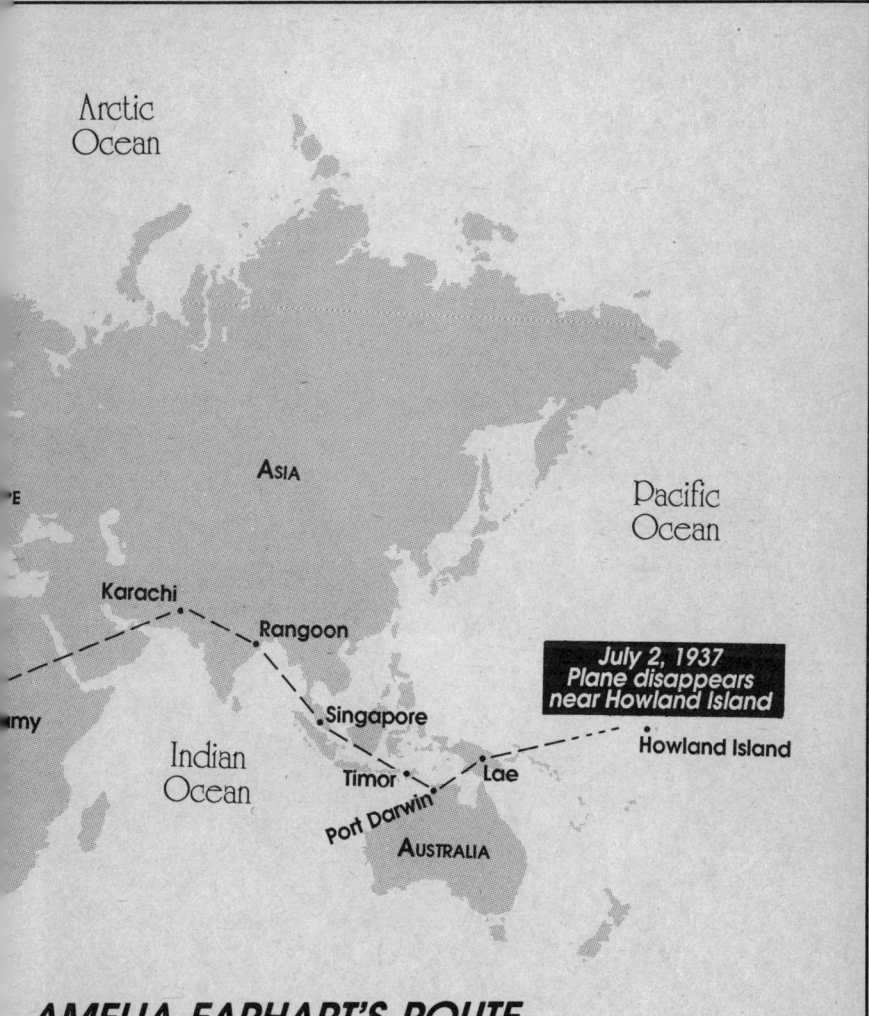

Amelia Earhart, while on layover during her first transatlantic trip on the *Friendship*. It was the flight that would make her famous. The Bettmann Archive

Chapter One

Mayday!

Amelia woke up early and struggled out of bed. She walked slowly to the bathroom of her hotel room. She rubbed her eyes and looked in the mirror, laughing at what she saw. There were white circles around her eyes from her flight goggles. The rest of her face was red and chapped from the wind, sun, and cold. There were deep gray circles under her red, swollen eyes. The rest of her face was pale and thin. Amelia raised her hand to her brow. She ran her finger over the wrinkles on her forehead and sighed. "I've been flying for weeks," she said to herself. "But to look at me, you'd think years had passed since I left home."

She splashed cold water on her face. Today she had to be especially alert. It was one of the

WHAT HAPPENED TO AMELIA EARHART?

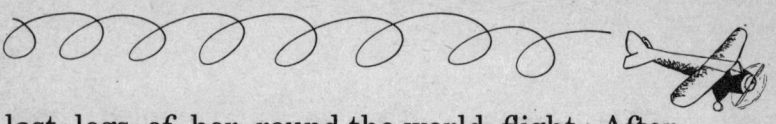

last legs of her round-the-world flight. After today, there was only one leg of the trip left. But today was the most dangerous part of the journey.

She quickly put on her usual flying clothes. Her well-worn brown pants were easy to move around in. Her simple white blouse fit neatly under her wrinkled leather flying jacket. Amelia wiped the dust from her goggles with a cloth. She carefully laid them next to her helmet and gloves. She slipped into her boots and headed out the door.

Amelia walked a few doors up the hallway and knocked. "Fred, are you awake? Want to join me for breakfast?"

There was no sound. "Fred, are you there?" she asked, knocking again. Fred Noonan was Amelia Earhart's navigator. He read the maps and instruments in the plane so that Amelia could stay on course. They needed to discuss today's tricky flight over the Pacific Ocean. Finally Amelia heard a thump and groan from the other side of Fred's door.

"I'm coming. I'm coming," Fred called. A few seconds later, he opened the door. Fred was fully

MAYDAY!

dressed, but his clothes were all rumpled. Amelia could see that he had slept in them. He rubbed his bleary eyes.

"You don't look so well, Fred. What's the matter?" Amelia asked.

"I don't feel too well either. I stayed up late with some other hotel guests. I think I had too much whiskey. I have an awful headache," Fred replied.

Fred and Amelia had been flying for days. Many times they flew ten to fifteen hours without stopping. The plane was small and cramped, and they could hardly move their legs. Both Amelia and Fred were worn out.

Fred Noonan and Amelia Earhart had left Miami, Florida, full of hope and energy on June 1. It was now July 2, 1937, and they had reached Lae, New Guinea, almost three-quarters of the way around the world. In one month, they had flown twenty-two thousand miles.

No one had ever come this far around the earth by plane. Today Fred and Amelia were taking off for a tiny island in the middle of the Pacific Ocean. It was called Howland Island, and it was almost impossible to see from the air.

WHAT HAPPENED TO AMELIA EARHART?

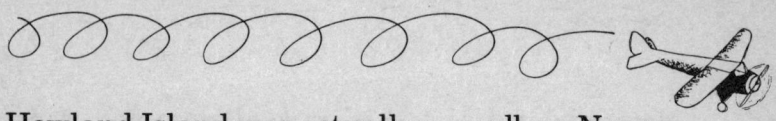

Howland Island was actually a sandbar. No one lived there. It had no buildings. The island was two miles long and three-quarters of a mile wide, and its highest point of elevation was only twenty-five feet. Howland Island was discovered by sailing ships over one hundred years before, and their reports were not very accurate.

Amelia knew Howland would not be easy to find, but she had no choice. It was as far as her plane could go. If she flew longer than twenty hours, she would run out of gas and only the ocean would be beneath them.

Amelia's Lockheed Electra 10E was normally a ten-passenger plane. All the seats had been removed. Half of the cabin was filled with extra fuel tanks. More tanks were added under each wing. Altogether, Amelia carried about one thousand gallons of fuel. The Electra had twin engines that could reach 550 horsepower each.

The other half of the cabin was for Fred. It held a large chart table for maps. There was a glass window in the table with a master compass underneath. Next to this table, there were several other instruments. There were three chronometers to keep exact time. There was an al-

MAYDAY!

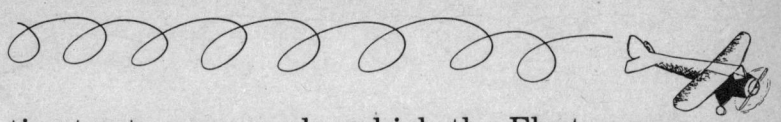

timeter to measure how high the Electra was flying. There was a temperature gauge and an air-speed indicator. Fred was tired of working with all the equipment in such a small space. He wanted longer layovers. He also wanted them more often. But Amelia always wanted to push on. She wanted to arrive back in the United States on the Fourth of July.

"I know how you feel, Fred," said Amelia that morning. There had been many sleepless nights in buggy, tropical climates. They both had gotten sick several times from eating strange foods and drinking bad water.

"I'm tired too," Amelia went on. "But after today, we will have almost made it to Hawaii. Then we can fly home."

"All right, all right," Fred grumbled. He felt too sick to eat breakfast, but he wearily prepared for the flight. Amelia hurried to the dining room. She had some juice, toast, and coffee. Amelia always ate little before a flight. While she was in the air, she hardly ate at all. Mostly, she took small sips from her thermos. She couldn't drink too much. There was no toilet in her little airplane. Besides, she had to stay in

WHAT HAPPENED TO AMELIA EARHART?

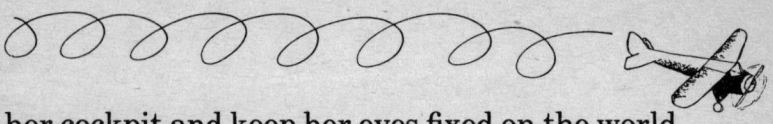

her cockpit and keep her eyes fixed on the world beneath and the skies ahead.

After breakfast, Amelia went back to her room for the last time. She packed her knapsack with a toothbrush, a comb, two handkerchiefs, a tube of cold cream, her books, some letters, and a pistol for firing distress signals. All of her clothes, in shades of brown, were in one small suitcase. She fastened the straps tightly and flung the knapsack over her shoulder. But she had second thoughts about weight. ["The lighter the plane is, the longer our fuel will last. A lighter plane flies faster too. Every little bit helps," Amelia considered.] She took off the knapsack and unloaded the books and the pistol. She refastened it and left.

Today's flight was dangerous in two ways. It was a long flight, and the destination was difficult. But besides that, the flight path was over enemy territory. It was 1937. The stirrings of World War II were felt everywhere. The Japanese military was expanding into the Pacific, and they controlled the Marshall Islands, right near Howland. If for some reason Amelia couldn't reach Howland Island, she might have

MAYDAY!

to land on a Japanese-controlled island. Today the United States and Japan are friends, but in 1937 they were not. No one knew what the Japanese would think, or how they would react. Amelia knew the risks. But she was driven by the dream of being the first woman to fly around the world.

Out in the hallway, Amelia ran into Fred. He was just leaving his room. As they drove to the airfield, they discussed their plans.

"We'll take off at ten A.M. exactly and head due east," said Fred. "Our timing has to be exact. That way we can use the position of the sun and stars to help guide us," he reminded Amelia. Fred Noonan was one of the best navigators in the world. He knew just what position the sun or stars would be in the sky at each hour of the day. If he knew the exact time, the pattern of stars in the sky at that hour would tell him their position in the air. Then they could correct their path if they were off course.

They had been delayed for four days. The weather had been very cloudy. Today the forecast was for some clouds and rain, but there was enough clear sky to take off. Amelia decided to

WHAT HAPPENED TO AMELIA EARHART?

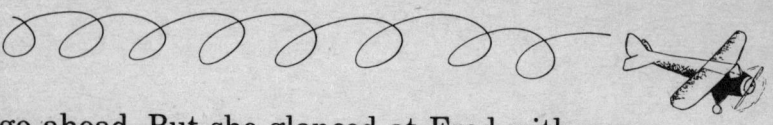

go ahead. But she glanced at Fred with a worried look. Maybe she was pushing too hard. He was the best navigator she could have, but today his eyes were so red and swollen!

"Fred's not our only guide," she thought. "Our radio equipment is in good working order. The crew of the Coast Guard ship *Itasca* will be tuned in to my plane. They will help keep our bearings so that we land safely on Howland Island. Besides, Fred has never failed me before."

A few minutes before ten, Amelia and Fred climbed into her plane, the Electra. Amelia paused on the wing. She waved and smiled to the crowd that had gathered to see her off. She breathed deeply and stepped into the cockpit. Amelia pulled her headphones down over her ears. She yanked her tight leather helmet on over her short hair. The engine roared. She felt the familiar hum of the motor. Amelia swung the plane around and looked out onto the runway. "This is it, Fred." He looked at her and managed a smile.

Meanwhile, more than twenty-five hundred miles away, Chief Radioman Bellarts settled into his seat aboard the ship *Itasca.* He snapped

MAYDAY!

his earphones into place and flicked on the radio switch. The *Itasca* was stationed just off Howland Island. Captain Thompson and his radiomen were Amelia's link to land. In 1937, radar had not been invented yet, so these men had the job of guiding her safely to Howland. Bellarts wiped his forehead with his handkerchief. He was already nervous. There had been confusion about Amelia's radio equipment. Captain Thompson asked Amelia which radio frequencies she preferred. He wanted to know her communication schedule at least twelve hours before she left Lae. The *Itasca* crew needed the time to set their equipment. They also had to notify the other Coast Guard ships, the *Ontario* and the *Swan,* of Amelia's radio frequencies. Those ships were also watching out for Amelia.

Captain Thompson heard back from Amelia. But he got two messages. One was directly from Amelia, asking the *Itasca* to broadcast at a very high frequency, but a message from Amelia's contacts in San Francisco said that her equipment wouldn't work in that range. Captain Thompson was not sure what frequencies she would be speaking on.

WHAT HAPPENED TO AMELIA EARHART?

"She has the best equipment available," he thought. "As long as we stay right at these controls, we'll be sure to keep in touch."

Back in New Guinea, radio operator Harry Balfour had arranged to have contact with Amelia every hour. He sat at his station waiting to hear her first transmission. Amelia would report her position and altitude on the radio. But bad weather could make it difficult to navigate. If the fliers got off course, they could radio for help. Operators on land and sea could direct them. Coast Guard boats could send up smoke signals. The smoke would help Amelia and Fred to see the boats. Then they would be guided to land. The radio was Amelia's lifeline.

Back on the runway, Amelia took a deep breath and rammed both throttles forward. At top speed, the plane was headed right for the Pacific Ocean. As they reached the very end of the runway, the plane shot up into the morning mist. Through the clouds, Amelia saw New Guinea. The jungle was like a soft and thick green blanket. She and Fred were airborne, and they had almost twenty hours of flying ahead. The crowd of reporters and fans back on the

MAYDAY!

ground watched as the pioneer aviator soared into the clouds and disappeared.

It was the last time anyone would ever see Amelia Earhart alive.

Amy and Edwin Earhart, Amelia's parents.
Schlesinger Library, Radcliffe College

Chapter Two

First Flight

"AMELIA MARY EARHART!" shouted Grandpa Otis. "What are you doing? Come down here right now!"

Seven-year-old Amelia climbed down from the shed roof. She faced her grandfather. For the past few months, Amelia and her five-year-old sister, Muriel, or "Pidge," as she was called, had been living in Kansas with their grandparents. Their father, Edwin Earhart, was a lawyer for the railroads. He had to travel a lot. This time, their mother went with him, so the girls were spending the summer with their grandparents.

Amelia's grandfather was a judge. He was always fair with 'Melia and Pidge. Today he would listen to 'Melia's explanation, as usual. But he was scared when he came outside and saw Amelia perched on the shed roof.

WHAT HAPPENED TO AMELIA EARHART?

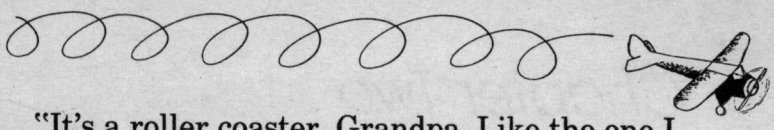

"It's a roller coaster, Grandpa. Like the one I saw at the World's Fair in St. Louis. It works really well. The other kids want to try it."

With the help of her sister, two cousins, Tootie and Katchie, and two neighborhood boys, Bailey and Jared, Amelia had built the roller coaster she pictured in her mind. They nailed two boards side by side to the shed roof, on one end. The boards slanted down so the ends rested on the ground. For her "car," 'Melia took the wheels off an old pair of roller skates. She hammered them onto the bottom of another board. It looked like the skateboards we use today.

Next, she climbed to the top of the shed roof. She put the roller-board between her legs and jumped down onto her homemade slide. Off she flew down the planks! She landed with a bang in the backyard. Grandma Otis heard the crash. Judge Otis came out to take a look. When he got there, 'Melia had already climbed back on the roof for a second try.

"That may be a lot of fun and it's certainly an unusual idea. But it's very dangerous!" warned Judge Otis. "Take it apart right now. You'll have to think of a new game. One that you play on the ground."

Six-year-old Amelia and her four-year-old sister Muriel ("Pidge") in a rare moment: all dressed up on the porch of their Grandpa and Grandma Otis's house in Atchison, Kansas. Schlesinger Library, Radcliffe College

Reluctantly Amelia agreed. Judge Otis shook his head and went back inside. That was Amelia: always ready for adventure. Amelia's grandmother became so hopeless of keeping 'Melia and Pidge clean, she let the girls wear bloomers instead of dresses. Bloomers were long, fancy undershorts, and Amelia loved them. They were perfect for playing outdoors. She wore them every day to collect insects. Other girls her age

15

WHAT HAPPENED TO AMELIA EARHART?

liked dolls. Amelia liked bugs. Her favorite book was *Insect Life*.

It wasn't surprising that Amelia was so adventurous. Her mother was the first woman to climb Pike's Peak, in Colorado. Grandma Otis had known adventure too. She and the judge were among the first pioneers. They had traveled west to settle in wild territory. The stories about their journey were Amelia's favorites. She wished that she had been a pioneer.

'Melia and Pidge looked forward to the return of their parents. But when they did return, it wasn't for long. Mr. Earhart still had to travel a lot. So Amelia and Pidge continued to live with their grandparents in Atchison, Kansas, for another year. Finally Edwin Earhart got a job with the claims department for the railroad in Des Moines, Iowa, and he wouldn't have to travel anymore. The girls were sorry to leave their happy home in Kansas. But they were glad to be living with their parents again.

For a while, life in the Earhart home was happy and full of love. Amelia did well in school, especially in math. When she was given a math problem, she could just figure for a minute in her head. Then she knew the answer!

FIRST FLIGHT

Amelia's father enjoyed his new job. He often had lunch with his coworkers. Sometimes he would have an alcoholic drink at these meals. For Edwin Earhart, this occasional drink led to a bad drinking problem. Drinking gave Amelia's father a bad temper. Amelia's mother and father began to fight a lot. Edwin Earhart did his work poorly and lost his job. The family began to have money problems. Amelia watched helplessly as her happy home became a place of anger and sadness.

When Amelia was sixteen, her church held a Christmas dance for the community's teenagers. Amelia and Pidge hadn't been invited to any parties since people in the town found out about their father's drinking problem. In those days, a girl couldn't go to a party unless her father escorted her. No one wanted a drunken man at their home. But this was a church party for everyone.

Amelia and Muriel were very excited. They dressed early and decorated the house. They planned to invite two boys over for hot chocolate after the dance. Mr. Earhart promised to be home at six o'clock to escort them.

The clock struck six, seven, then eight o'clock.

WHAT HAPPENED TO AMELIA EARHART?

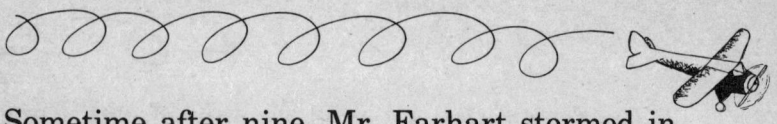

Sometime after nine, Mr. Earhart stormed in through the door, drunk. Muriel burst into tears and ran to her room. But Amelia just gave her father a cold stare.

Missing the party was not the biggest disappointment for Amelia, but she was hurt because her father had broken his promise, again. As she carefully placed the china cups back in the cupboard, she thought, "I don't ever want to feel this way again. I'll make a better life and I'll have nothing to be ashamed of." She raised her head and said out loud to herself, "When people say the name Amelia Earhart, it will be with admiration and respect."

Although Amelia still loved her father, after the Christmas party incident, things changed. She didn't look up to him anymore.

As Amelia grew older, she believed more than ever that girls could do anything boys could. Girls could be doctors and lawyers. They could even be pilots! Amelia worked hard to be an outstanding student and an important member of the basketball team. While other girls her age began to think about marriage, Amelia thought only about a career. She graduated from high school in 1916. Her mother wanted Amelia and

FIRST FLIGHT

Pidge to attend good colleges. Amy Earhart enrolled her daughters in private preparatory schools. Amelia went to the Ogontz School in Philadelphia. Pidge went to school in Toronto.

Amelia missed her sister in Canada. She decided to visit Pidge during Christmas vacation. The trip gave Amelia a real shock. As she walked the streets of Toronto, Amelia saw men in wheelchairs and on crutches everywhere. Some were even missing an arm or a leg. The effects of the World War in Europe were all around.

"I can't believe my eyes, Pidge!" exclaimed Amelia. "We don't see anything like this in the United States. And all of these men will never be the same," she added. "I just have to help."

Within days, Amelia was settled in Toronto and working at a local hospital. She was a nurse's aide, helping to care for the wounded soldiers. Some of the men had been army pilots. When they left the hospital, Amelia often went to the airfield to visit them. Very soon, she was visiting to see the planes as much as to see her new friends.

In the fall of 1919 she started at Columbia University in New York City. Amelia planned to be a doctor, but she soon decided that medicine

Amelia as a nurse's aide in Toronto during the First World War. It was during her time in Toronto that Amelia first became interested in flying.
Schlesinger Library, Radcliffe College

FIRST FLIGHT

and college weren't for her. Her mother urged Amelia to join her and her father, and Amelia went to California, where her parents were now living.

One afternoon, shortly after arriving in California, Amelia and her father went to an air circus. Stunt flying was popular and drew big crowds. At that time, few people had actually gone up in a plane, but Amelia decided then and there she *had* to fly. She had her first ride with Frank Hawks, who later became a famous pilot himself. Amelia held her breath as they flew over California. She couldn't believe the beauty of the landscape from the sky. The blue ocean, the green mountains, and the golden sands made a stunning picture. And in the sky, she felt so free. She could soar above all the troubles of the world.

"Imagine all the places we could go...." Amelia thought as they came in for a landing. "Think of what a different world it would be if we could visit one another in countries all over the earth."

As she walked off the landing field, Amelia calmly approached her father. "I think I'd like to take flying lessons," she said. But in her heart

WHAT HAPPENED TO AMELIA EARHART?

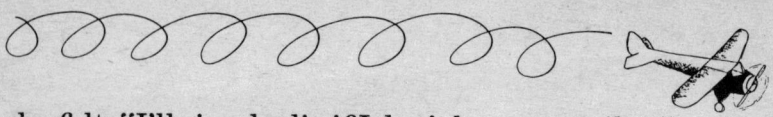

she felt, "I'll simply die if I don't become a pilot."

Amelia persuaded her father to pay for a few lessons. But in those days it was considered improper for a young woman to spend too much time alone with a man, so Amelia signed up for flying lessons with the only woman pilot available, Neta Snook. After her first lesson, Amelia was hooked. Her goal in life was to fly at all costs, and nothing could stop her. She worked twenty-eight different jobs. She sold sausage and drove a truck. She would do anything to continue to fly. The cost of lessons, fuel, and plane upkeep was very high. All of Amelia's money went toward learning to fly. At times she could barely afford to eat, but Amelia was determined. By the time she was twenty-three years old, she had earned enough money to buy her own airplane for two thousand dollars. It was painted bright yellow and she proudly named it the *Canary*.

Amelia struggled to pay for her expensive hobby of flying. But in April of 1927, that all changed. One day she received a phone call from Captain Hilton Railey—a stranger with an interesting proposal. It was a proposal that would change her life.

Amelia and her first plane, a bright yellow Kinner Canary. She bought it in 1922 for $2,000 and aptly named it the *Canary*.
Schlesinger Library, Radcliffe College

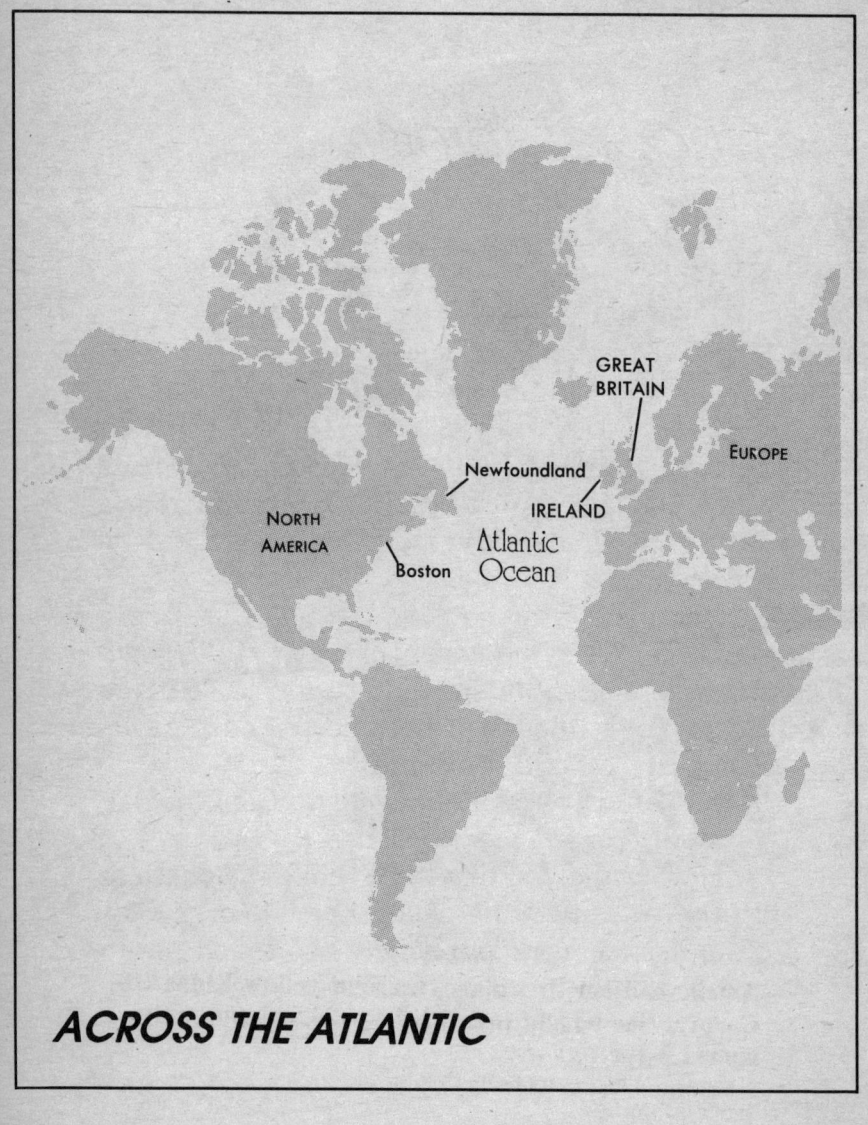

Chapter Three
Across the Atlantic

"Miss Earhart, I have been asked to contact you," Captain Railey began. "I'm organizing a very exciting and dangerous flight. Are you interested?"

"Perhaps," Amelia said evenly. The mere mention of a flying adventure sent chills down Amelia's spine. But she didn't want to seem too eager. She wanted to present herself as someone who made careful decisions.

That afternoon Amelia went to Captain Railey's office to get more details.

"How would you like to be the first woman to fly the Atlantic?" he asked her. "George Putnam, a New York publisher, has asked me to find a woman to make the flight. First, I'd like to know more about your background."

WHAT HAPPENED TO AMELIA EARHART?

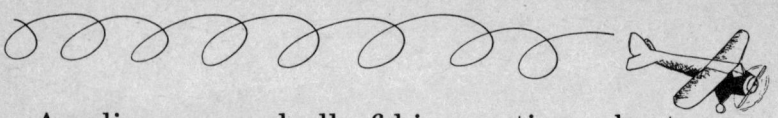

Amelia answered all of his questions about her education, upbringing, and flying experience. Captain Railey was very impressed. Amelia was warm and friendly, yet polite and dignified. Two weeks later, Amelia had another interview. This time the interview was in New York City. The details of the flight were explained to her.

Mrs. Amy Guest, a very rich American woman, wanted to sponsor a flight across the Atlantic Ocean. She was married to the Honorable Frederick Guest, son of an English Lord. She wanted the flight to be made in a plane called the *Friendship*. The flight would be a symbol of good relations between England and America. Mrs. Guest wanted a woman to be on the plane. She must be a pilot, well educated, attractive, and very well mannered.

Two well-known men in aviation, Bill Stultz and Lou Gordon, would also make the flight. Stultz was a pilot and navigator. Gordon was a copilot and flight mechanic. The woman chosen to make the flight would go along as a passenger.

"This is a great chance for people to take notice of the women in flying," thought Amelia.

ACROSS THE ATLANTIC

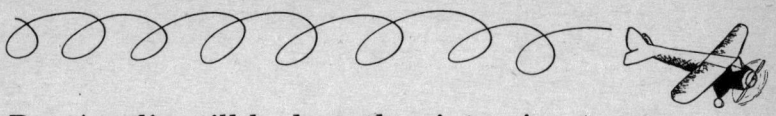

But Amelia still had another interview to pass before a decision could be made. This one was with George Putnam.

When Amelia met with Mr. Putnam, he thought she looked just like a female Charles Lindbergh, the world-famous pilot.

"Why, this is too good to be true," thought George. "It's a Lady Lindy. The public will love her." George Putnam was a successful writer and publisher of adventure stories. He knew what people liked to read about. He was also a good publicity agent. He knew how to draw attention to people and events.

Back in Boston, the next two days seemed like forever. Finally she received a call from George Putnam. She had been chosen as commander/passenger on the *Friendship*. The job was not paid, but if the flight was a success, she'd be famous. Then Amelia could go on tours and give lectures. She could write articles for magazines and newspapers and be paid well.

Amelia was practical. She could see this was a good chance for fame and fortune. But she was also a pioneer. She would have made the flight no matter what.

WHAT HAPPENED TO AMELIA EARHART?

The plans for the flight were made in secret. It was important to make sure that no one else made the flight before the *Friendship*. Amelia had to be the first. Not even Amelia's family knew that she was about to become the first woman to cross the Atlantic Ocean by air.

Weeks passed while she and the crew waited in Boston. The flight was in two stages. First they would fly to Newfoundland. From there, they would cross the Atlantic. But when the weather was clear in Boston, there was fog in Newfoundland. When skies were clear in Newfoundland, it was foggy in Boston. The crew needed clear skies for the whole trip. George Putnam waited with Amelia. The two spent a lot of time together and became good friends. Amelia gave him the nickname "G.P.," and he called her "A.E."

Finally, on June 3, 1928, the weather was perfect. Skies were clear. There was enough wind to help lift them off the pontoons in the water. Would this be the day they took off or just another dress rehearsal?

Bill Stultz, the pilot, pointed the *Friendship* into the wind and opened the throttles. The

ACROSS THE ATLANTIC

plane hardly moved. They tossed off six of the eight cans of gas they carried for emergencies. Stultz opened the throttles again, but the plane was still too heavy. Lew Gower, the backup pilot, silently and sadly gathered his belongings. He stepped off the plane onto a launch. With Amelia, Bill, and Lou Gordon on board, it took only sixty-seven seconds for the *Friendship* to get airborne.

But their trials were not over yet. They reached Trepassey Bay, Newfoundland, on June 4. By now the public knew about the flight. Thousands followed news reports of these aviators. For many days there was no news. The fog was so thick in Trepassey, they couldn't take off. It was cold. Their clothes were dirty after many days of wear. The three aviators were tired of playing cards and waiting.

At last, on June 18, the weather report was good. They had a successful takeoff. But there was other bad news. Mabel Boll, another pilot, was trying to beat Amelia. She was trying to take the record as the first woman to make a transatlantic crossing.

This long delay had given Mabel a head start.

WHAT HAPPENED TO AMELIA EARHART?

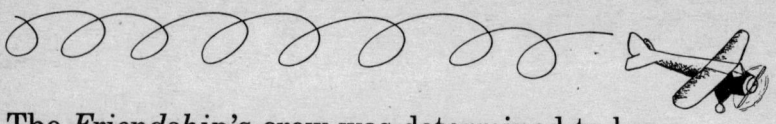

The *Friendship*'s crew was determined to keep going no matter what. They flew through bad weather conditions. More than once, Amelia was afraid of dying. After twenty hours and forty-nine minutes of flying, they were almost out of fuel. Exhausted, they had to land.

"Ship ahoy!" called a startled fisherman passing the afternoon in his boat. It was certainly strange to see a plane on the water. "Who are you folks and where did you come from?"

Stultz leaned out the window. He was almost too tired to speak. "We've just flown across the Atlantic!" he yelled. "What part of Ireland are we in?"

"Ireland?!" cried the fisherman. "You're in the south of Wales!" They had lost their bearings, but they had made it across the ocean!

As they spoke, a small fleet of boats gathered around the plane. Amelia greeted the curious sailors while Bill Stultz went ashore to radio George Putnam that they had arrived safely. Within a few hours the American people heard the news. They cheered "Lady Lindy" and the *Friendship*.

The next morning, Stultz awoke to find a huge

ACROSS THE ATLANTIC

sack outside his hotel room door. He ran to the next room and knocked on Amelia's door.

"Look at this!" he cried. "Telegrams, hundreds of them!"

Amelia reached into the bag. She pulled out a yellow envelope and stared at it. Slowly, carefully, she opened it. In short gasps, she read aloud:

TO YOU THE FIRST WOMAN SUCCESSFULLY TO SPAN THE NORTH ATLANTIC BY AIR THE GREAT ADMIRATION OF MYSELF AND THE UNITED STATES.

SIGNED,
PRESIDENT CALVIN COOLIDGE

Amelia watched as Stultz and Gordon gleefully opened telegrams. A little voice whispered inside her head. "You were the first woman . . . but you didn't fly the plane. . . ."

She had an idea. "The next time I get a telegram from the president," she thought, "it will be for flying across the Atlantic. Only this time, *I'll* be the pilot, and I'll do it *alone*."

Amelia with her husband and chief promoter, George Putnam The Bettmann Archive

Chapter Four
Floating on Air

Amelia's Atlantic crossing brought her instant fame. She went on a publicity tour. George Putnam went too. Amelia told him her dream of crossing the Atlantic solo. George thought it was a good goal. But he suggested she make an overland flight first.

"A transcontinental flight from California to New York would be a record," George offered.

Amelia thought for a moment. "Yes, and I'll make the flight in an autogiro!" In 1931 an autogiro was considered a crazy flying machine. It was half plane and half helicopter. Amelia was the only woman flying one at the time.

So again the team of Earhart and Putnam began to plan for Amelia's next challenge. Around the same time, they began to prepare for their wedding.

WHAT HAPPENED TO AMELIA EARHART?

The two were a natural match. Spending so much time together, they had fallen in love. George supported Amelia's career, and he was a big part of it. This was very important to Amelia. Yet she was worried. Was marriage the right step for an aviator? Few women of the early 1930s had a career. Amelia's was especially different. Practically no women combined a career and marriage.

One day before Amelia married George, she reached into her desk and took out a sheet of paper. "Dear G.P.," she began. She wrote to him about her worries. Amelia told George that she wanted to be a loving partner. But her career came first.

> Let us not interfere with the other's work or play.... I must exact a cruel promise, and that is you will let me go in a year if we find no happiness together.
>
> I will try to do my best in every way and give you that part of me you know and seem to want.
>
> A.E.

FLOATING ON AIR

On February 7, 1931, Amelia Earhart and George Putnam were married. It was a small and quiet ceremony. Amelia's career went on as planned. The couple knew that danger was always around the corner. Every time Amelia climbed into a cockpit and they kissed each other good-bye, they knew it could be for the last time.

Amelia's flight across America was a success, so just months after their marriage, G.P. and A.E. prepared for Amelia's solo Atlantic flight.

On a lovely May morning, Amelia took her last walk for a while. She roamed among the trees and flowers of her calm country home. George paced anxiously on the patio. Later that day they would say good-bye.

As the sun set that afternoon, Amelia took off into a sky of brilliant colors. At first, all went well. Then she noticed that her altimeter wasn't working! The altimeter told her how high she was flying. Now she would have to judge by eyesight. It was nighttime, and it would be difficult and dangerous. If she flew too high, the cold air would form ice on her wings. Then the plane would be hard to control.

WHAT HAPPENED TO AMELIA EARHART?

 Amelia stayed calm. But a short while later, the sky lit up. The plane began to shake. She was flying right through a lightning storm! Soon after, the plane began to vibrate. A seam in the plane's body had come apart! Amelia saw flames roaring against the night sky! There was a fire in one of the exhaust vents! But it was too late to turn back. Besides, Amelia wouldn't think of it.

Next, she flew into heavy clouds. She couldn't see anything. She decided to fly on top of the clouds. But without her altimeter, she didn't know how high she was climbing. The plane began to feel heavy and slow.

"I must have ice on the wings," she gasped, and the plane began to spin. Amelia gripped the controls and tried desperately to steady it. As she spun to a lower altitude, the ice melted. The plane was level again. Amelia looked down and saw the whitecaps of the stormy ocean just below! Quickly she aimed upward and narrowly missed the wild waves.

All night, Amelia flew the Lockheed Vega, trying to keep above the fog but below the ice. She sniffed her bottle of smelling salts often to

FLOATING ON AIR

keep awake. When the sun finally rose, she heaved a sigh of relief.

Amelia couldn't relax for long. Suddenly she felt something dripping on her left shoulder. It was gasoline! And it was leaking into the cockpit! The vibration caused by the split seam was getting worse, and Amelia knew there were still flames burning there. What if the leaking fuel reached those flames? It would explode! She and her plane would be demolished!

"I have to land right away," thought a terrified Amelia. "At the first sight of land, I'll bring the plane down. I only hope it won't be too late. . . ."

Amelia flew for two more hours. Finally she sighted land. But there was no landing field. She had to land the plane in the nearest pasture. Amelia carefully guided the plane down. She didn't want to hit any cows down below.

As soon as she was safely down, Amelia turned off every switch. She quickly got out of the plane. Standing before her was a very surprised farmhand. He stared at her. His mouth hung open.

"Where am I?" asked the exhausted Amelia.

Amelia greeted by the crowd in Londonderry, Ireland, in 1931, after her triumphant solo flight across the Atlantic.
The Bettmann Archive

"In Gallagher's pasture, near Londonderry, in Northern Ireland," said Danny McCallion. He didn't know if Amelia was a man or woman. In her flying clothes and helmet, it was hard to tell. "Have you come far?"

"From America," she replied. "For the last fifteen hours I've had only a can of tomato juice

FLOATING ON AIR

to drink and nothing to eat. Is there somewhere I might get a drink of water?"

Danny led her to Gallagher's farmhouse. When Amelia explained who she was, Mr. Gallagher alerted the police. In less than an hour, telegraph lines were buzzing all around the world. News of Amelia's safe arrival in Ireland made world history!

A reporter telephoned George. He was relieved and ecstatic. "Tell her to telephone me wherever she is; all I want is to hear her voice and tell her she is the greatest woman in the world. . . ." Amelia had done it! She had flown the Atlantic alone. She was more famous than she had imagined. She received honors and appointments beyond her dreams.

"To Amelia Earhart, the National Geographic Gold Medal." The assembly hall rang with applause.

"To Amelia Earhart, Honorary Membership in the National Aeronautics Association." The crowd cheered.

"To Amelia Earhart, the Harmon Trophy as America's Outstanding Woman." The audience shouted hurrah.

WHAT HAPPENED TO AMELIA EARHART?

This time she didn't get a congratulatory telegram from the president. She received a formal invitation to dine at the White House with President Roosevelt and the first lady!

Her success crossing the Atlantic only drove Amelia to set more records. In 1935, she was the first person to fly solo across the Pacific Ocean from Hawaii to California. The Mexican government invited Amelia to make the first solo flight from Los Angeles to Mexico. Amelia accepted. The flight was a success. Mexico issued a special postage stamp in honor of the trip.

Amelia's achievements went on. She opened a flying school and charter business. She was appointed as a consulting professor at Purdue University. *Cosmopolitan* magazine asked her to write articles for them. She even designed a line of practical clothing for women.

Amelia was a woman of many talents. She proved this to the world. But it was not enough for her.

"George," she said one morning as she sipped her orange juice. He looked up over his newspaper.

"I think I'd like to fly around the world."

The airport in Oakland, California, minutes after Amelia set a new record for first solo flight from Hawaii to California. She was swamped by over 10,000 well-wishers! AP/Wide World Photos

George put down the newspaper. He heaved a heavy sigh and rolled his eyes toward the sky. What else could he do but help Amelia begin planning her next flight?

*June 1, 1937
Earhart leaves Miami*

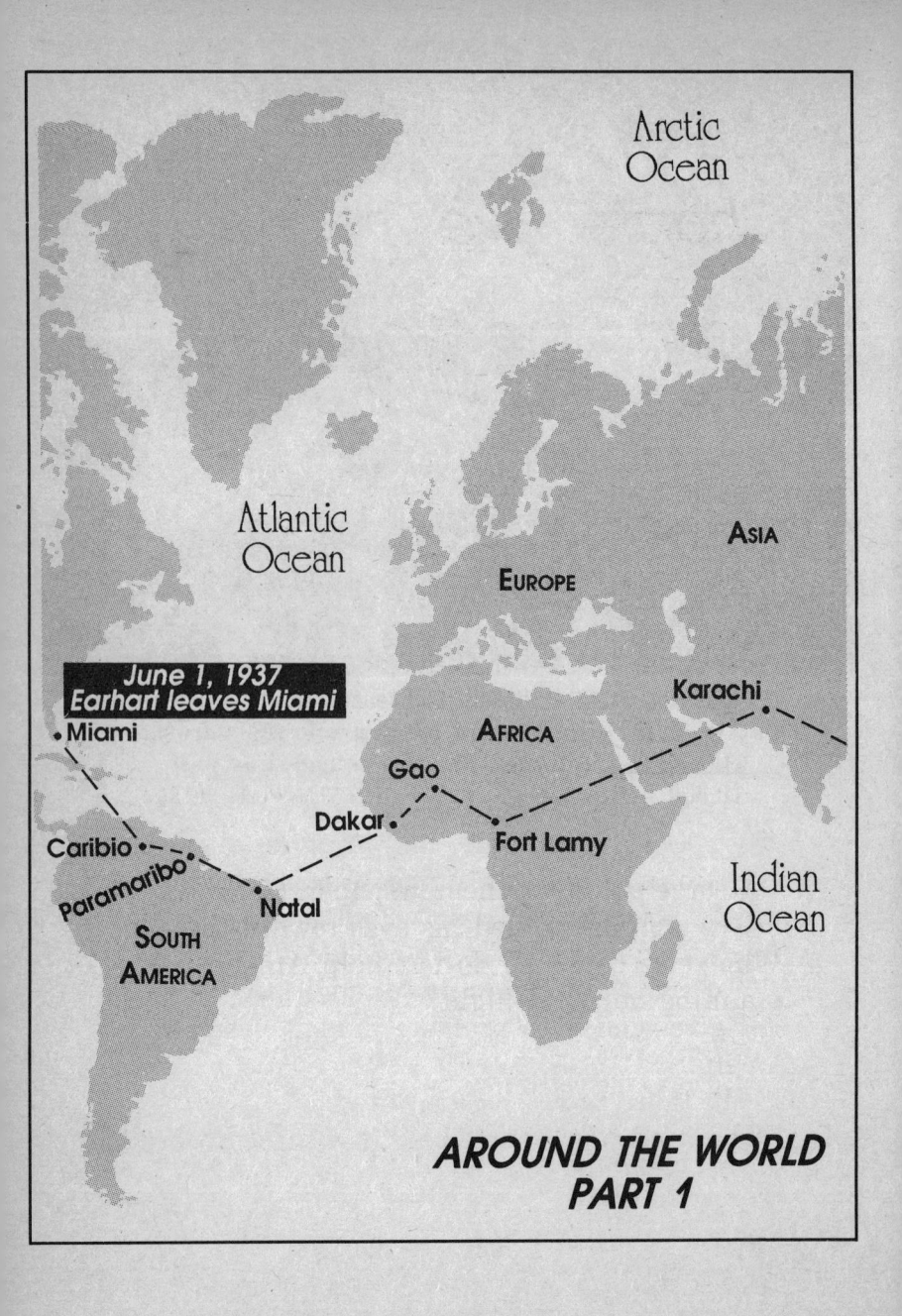

**AROUND THE WORLD
PART 1**

Chapter Five

Around the World

One afternoon as Amelia and George strolled through their garden, George said, "It will cost a fortune, you know."

Amelia knew just what George was talking about, although he had not mentioned the flight. And she did know it would be costly. Before she had a chance to reply, George continued.

"We'll need to set up some kind of fund. A cause people will donate to. I propose we set up the 'Amelia Earhart Fund for Aeronautical Research.' If you keep data on all aspects of the flight, it will benefit the whole field of aviation."

"Do you think there are enough people who will give money to promote flying?" wondered Amelia.

"We'll see to it," he answered.

The fund was established. It was set up with

WHAT HAPPENED TO AMELIA EARHART?

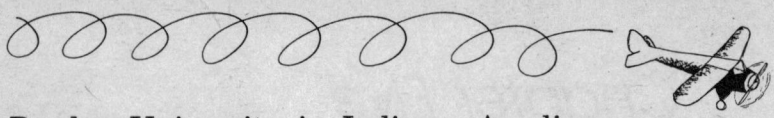

Purdue University in Indiana. Amelia was a consultant in Purdue's department for the study of careers for women. Amelia and George went to a dinner at the home of Dr. Edward Elliot, the president of Purdue. Amelia talked about her dreams for women and flying. Dr. Elliot had similar ideas. They talked about a plane as a "flying laboratory." Another guest, David Ross, became very excited. He promised to donate fifty thousand dollars. More donations in cash and equipment came in.

The Amelia Earhart Fund for Aeronautical Research raised eighty thousand dollars. The goal was to develop scientific and engineering data. That information would help to further the flying industry. Some of the money was used to buy the Electra 10E. Amelia would be flying over water much of the time. She would need to be in contact with radiomen on land and in boats. They would help her keep her direction. They could notify her of weather conditions ahead. If she needed help, she'd radio to people below to find out where she could land quickly and safely. Amelia used the rest of the money to add special navigational and radio equipment to the plane.

Amelia *(left)* **with First Lady Eleanor Roosevelt, who became a good friend.** The Bettmann Archive

After buying the Lockheed, Amelia needed permission from governments around the world. She'd have to land several times in foreign countries to refuel, and each country had to agree to this. Amelia had made good friends with Eleanor Roosevelt, the first lady, so she asked Mrs. Roosevelt to use her influence to help. Mrs. Roosevelt was glad to do so.

Still, it was difficult to decide the Electra's route around the world. Amelia chose to fly west, starting in California and heading out

WHAT HAPPENED TO AMELIA EARHART?

over the Pacific. But finding places to refuel was a problem. The airplanes of the 1930s didn't hold as much fuel or fly as fast as planes do today. She couldn't stay airborne for more than twenty hours. In that time, she couldn't cross the Pacific. She would need to land on a small island in the Pacific. These were not well charted in 1937. She couldn't be sure exactly where any of the islands were. Still, she would have to come down.

Amelia would be able to make the first leg of the flight, from California to Honolulu, in less than twenty hours. But where should Amelia land next? The Department of Commerce agreed to make a landing strip on tiny Howland Island. It was halfway from Hawaii to New Guinea. Amelia could refuel there.

After these plans were made, Amelia realized she would need an expert navigator. The navigator would help Amelia stay on course and land safely.

"Fred Noonan's got the best reputation around," Paul Mantz told Amelia. Paul was a good friend of Amelia's. They ran a flying school and charter business together. Paul was going to fly with Amelia as far as Honolulu.

AROUND THE WORLD

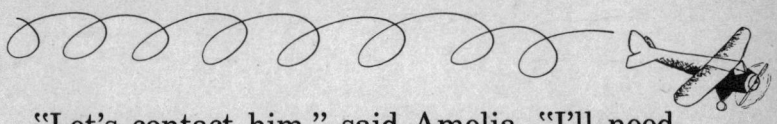

"Let's contact him," said Amelia. "I'll need the best there is. I hope he wants to take the risk."

Luckily, Fred Noonan was enthusiastic about the flight. It would be good for his career and good for aviation. On March 17, 1937, pilots Amelia Earhart and Paul Mantz, radioman Harry Manning, and navigator Fred Noonan boarded the Lockheed Electra. Crowds cheered in Oakland, California, as the crew waved goodbye. Radio audiences held their breath as they waited for news of these pioneers.

In just under sixteen hours, they landed safely on Honolulu. The first leg of the flight was over. But there had been some problems. The radio generator had burned out. It must be repaired before they took off for Howland Island. Paul Mantz stayed with Amelia until repairs were made. Then, on March 20, Amelia, Harry, and Fred took off again. Fred would go as far as Howland Island. His navigating skills would be essential. Harry planned to continue with Amelia to help her with radio contacts. He'd go as far as Australia. Amelia would return the rest of the way alone.

They never made it that far. Ten seconds

WHAT HAPPENED TO AMELIA EARHART?

before takeoff, the crowd gasped and screamed. The right wing of the plane dropped! The Electra spun around on the ground. The plane's bottom collapsed. The plane skidded along the runway on its belly. The sky was showered with sparks. Fuel poured out everywhere. Amelia acted quickly. She cut all the switches so the engine would be off. That way, the plane wouldn't burst into flames. The three were lucky. They all survived.

Some saw the accident as a bad sign. They tried to talk Amelia into quitting her flight. But Amelia laughed it off. She said that while the crash was still happening, she had decided to continue. Nothing could stop Amelia!

Amelia immediately began plans to try again. This time she'd fly east, leaving from Miami, Florida. Weather conditions would be better flying that way.

"But, Amelia," said an anxious George Putnam, "if you fly eastward, the landing on Howland Island will be almost the *last* leg of the trip. You'll be exhausted by then. Shouldn't you make the most dangerous landing when you're still fresh?"

"That's true," answered Amelia. "But there

George Putnam says good-bye to his wife before Amelia departs from Miami on June 1, 1937. She would disappear over the Pacific Ocean less than a month later. It would be the last time George Putnam saw his wife alive. UPI/Bettmann Newsphotos

WHAT HAPPENED TO AMELIA EARHART?

are many things to consider. Weather is one of the most important. Besides, I can rest in New Guinea a few extra days if I'm too worn-out."

"I'll trust your judgment," said George. He felt very somber. He had almost lost his wife on that first attempt. But he couldn't stand in her way. Amelia's mind was made up.

On June 1, 1937, the Electra was ready again for takeoff. The weather conditions were perfect in Miami. Before dawn, Amelia said her goodbyes to husband George before she and Fred boarded the plane one more time. A small crowd was gathered to see them off. This time they avoided publicity. They didn't want another failed attempt to make the headlines.

As the sun rose, the Electra flew east toward San Juan, Puerto Rico. The sun danced on the blue Atlantic Ocean. The sandy beaches of Puerto Rico glistened. How Amelia loved this view of the world from the sky!

The twosome of Earhart and Noonan continued on. They stopped to refuel several times in South America before they crossed the Atlantic again. Their next stop was Dakar, in Africa.

As she saw the thin line of the purple African coast, the fishing line over her shoulder began to

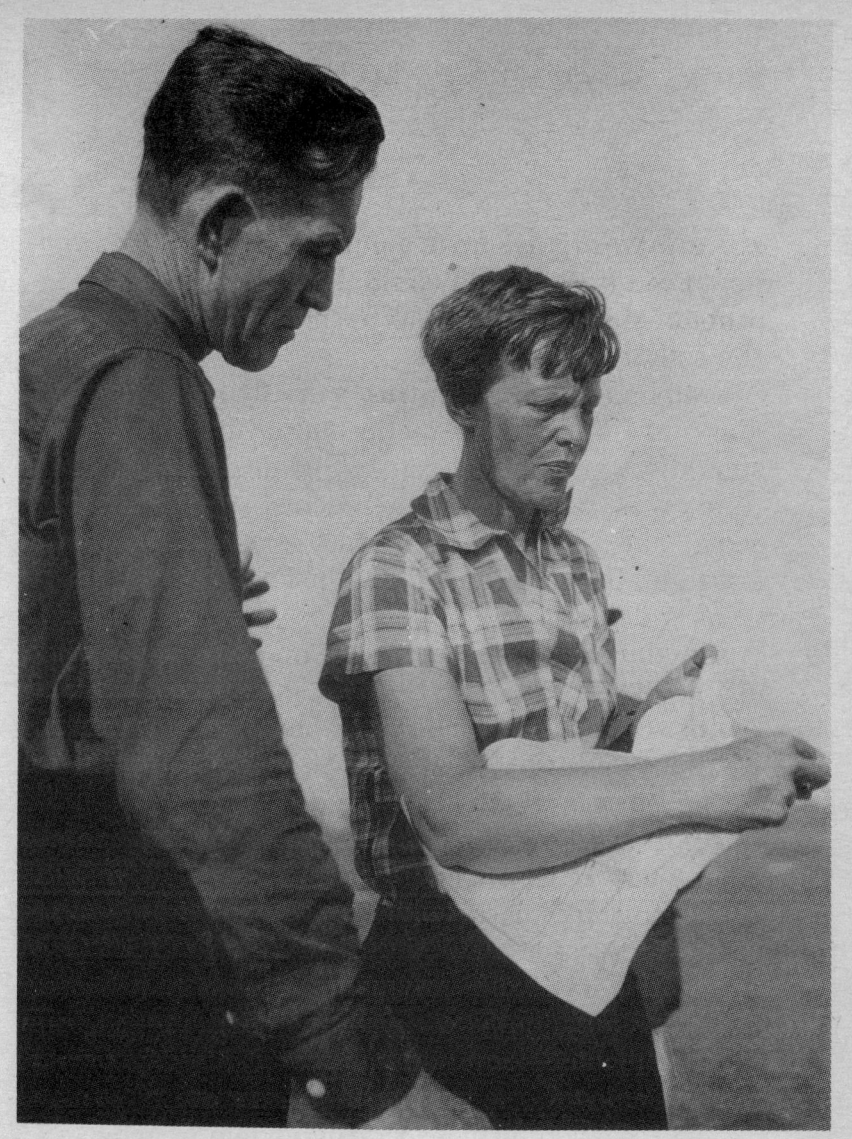

Amelia consults with her navigator, Fred Noonan, before taking off for Dakar, Africa.
UPI/Bettmann Newsphotos

WHAT HAPPENED TO AMELIA EARHART?

move. It was rigged up to a pulley system. That's how Fred and Amelia could pass notes to each other during a flight. It was too noisy to talk over the sound of the engines.

Fred had written that they were flying too far north of Dakar. But Amelia had a hunch they should stay north, not south. She decided to ignore Fred's note. When she reached the African coast, she turned left instead of right. They ended up in Senegal, not Dakar. Fred's calculations were correct.

Amelia's mistake was not a major one. But she had been stubborn. She felt she didn't need her navigator. Would she be stubborn once more on their way to Howland Island?

They flew across Africa over fields of zebra, tigers, and elephants running wild. Amelia felt as free as these magnificent creatures. They made stops in Africa, staying close to the equator. They went on to Sudan and then Ethiopia on the shores of the Red Sea. They crossed the Red Sea and the Arabian Sea to Karachi, Pakistan. The next stop was Calcutta and then Rangoon, Burma. Then Singapore, to what is now Indonesia. Next they went to Australia and on to Lae, New Guinea. They had completed twenty-

AROUND THE WORLD

two thousand miles of the flight. They were several days behind schedule because of weather. But it was almost over.

Amelia's thoughts turned to home and family. She was weary. She longed to walk quietly through the garden with her husband.

On July 2, she and Fred were ready to take off from Lae to Howland Island. With seven thousand miles to go, they were about to begin the most dangerous part of their flight. After Howland, they'd go on to Honolulu. Then they would head home to the mainland United States. As she ate breakfast, Amelia caught a glimpse of herself in a mirror. She hardly recognized herself. Her eyes were bloodshot. Her cheeks were swollen. She hadn't felt well in weeks.

Amelia looked away from her startling image. She turned the other way and stared out the hotel window.

"When this flight is over, I'm going to hang up my helmet and goggles," she mused. "I think I'm ready to keep my feet on the ground. Maybe it's time to start a family... to have children. Won't George be surprised to hear me say that!" She smiled to herself. She took one last sip of coffee and went to meet Fred.

WHAT HAPPENED TO AMELIA EARHART?

At 10:00 A.M. in Lae, New Guinea, a weary Amelia and a sick Fred boarded the Electra again. At the same moment, the radio crew of the Coast Guard ship *Itasca* put on their earphones. Click, click, click, went radio switches. Chief Radioman Bellarts checked the controls. Despite the earlier confusion over the radio frequency, all equipment was ready to guide Amelia to Howland Island.

Twelve hours and forty-two minutes later, Commander Warner Thompson, the *Itasca*'s captain, wrote in the ship's log, "*Itasca* to San Francisco: Have not heard Earhart signals up to this time but see no cause for concern as plane is still 1000 miles away." It was 1:12 A.M. at Howland.

At 2:30 *Itasca* heard from Amelia. There was so much static, they couldn't understand her. Leo Bellarts began to sweat. He wiped his brow and blew his nose. Would they be able to establish good radio contact? Earhart and Noonan's lives depended on it.

The hours crept by. The ship continued to send weather reports. The skies were partly cloudy and overcast. Amelia broke in on the

AROUND THE WORLD

radio phone. Each time she did, they couldn't make out her signals!

Finally, at 6:15 A.M., after almost eighteen hours in the air, Amelia's voice came through.

"I can hear her!" shouted Bellarts to the rest of the *Itasca* crew. "She wants her bearings."

"About two hundred miles out," continued Amelia. She had decided to whistle so they could figure out her location better. "Whistling now."

"Can you make her out?" asked Captain Thompson. He was very worried. Communications hadn't been going well.

"Yes, but not very well," answered Bellarts. "I'll send her a weather report. Then she'll know what to expect at Howland."

Bellarts sent the report to Earhart and Noonan. No answer.

"*Itasca* to Earhart. Please acknowledge our signal." No answer. Radioman Bellarts's eyes darted to the captain. They stared at each other. Would they be able to contact Amelia again?

At 6:45 her voice came through. "Please take bearing on us and report in half hour. I will make noise in microphone—about one hundred miles out."

WHAT HAPPENED TO AMELIA EARHART?

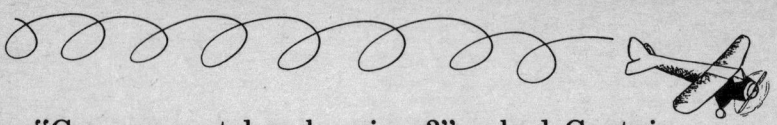

"Can you get her bearings?" asked Captain Thompson.

"She came through, but only for a minute. It wasn't long enough to get her location," replied Bellarts. He wiped his sweaty brow.

He began to shout into the microphone. The crew felt desperate. *"Itasca* to Earhart. Please come in!" No answer.

"Can you read me, Earhart?" Nothing.

Meanwhile, somewhere above the *Itasca,* Amelia clutched the controls of the Electra. She breathed deeply. She was trying to calm herself. Fred passed her a note. "Have they given you our bearings yet?"

"I don't think they hear me. I can't see them below. Are we near Howland?"

Fred crawled into the cockpit so they could talk to each other. "We should be on them," he answered. "So why can't they get our bearings?" Amelia chewed her lower lip. She looked at the gas gauge. After nineteen hours in the air, they were almost out of gas. Fred saw the gauge also. They looked at each other in silence for a moment. "I'll try again," said Amelia, shaking.

AROUND THE WORLD

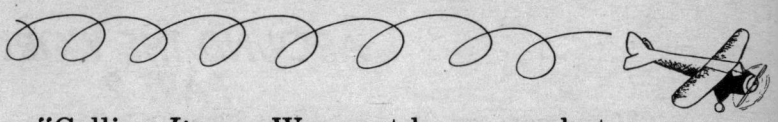

"Calling *Itasca*. We must be on you but cannot see you. Gas is running low. Only a half hour left. Been unable to reach you by radio."

No answer from *Itasca*.

At 8:00 A.M. Amelia radioed again: "We are circling but cannot hear you." No response. Amelia began to panic.

At 8:44 A.M., after twenty hours and seventeen minutes in the air, Amelia called: "We are running north and south but cannot see you! Come in, *Itasca*!"

She waited, terror-stricken, for word from Bellarts. Meanwhile, the desperate radioman shouted on every frequency. Earhart and Noonan never heard him. Or if they did, they couldn't reply.

That was the last time anyone heard Amelia Earhart's voice. The line was dead.

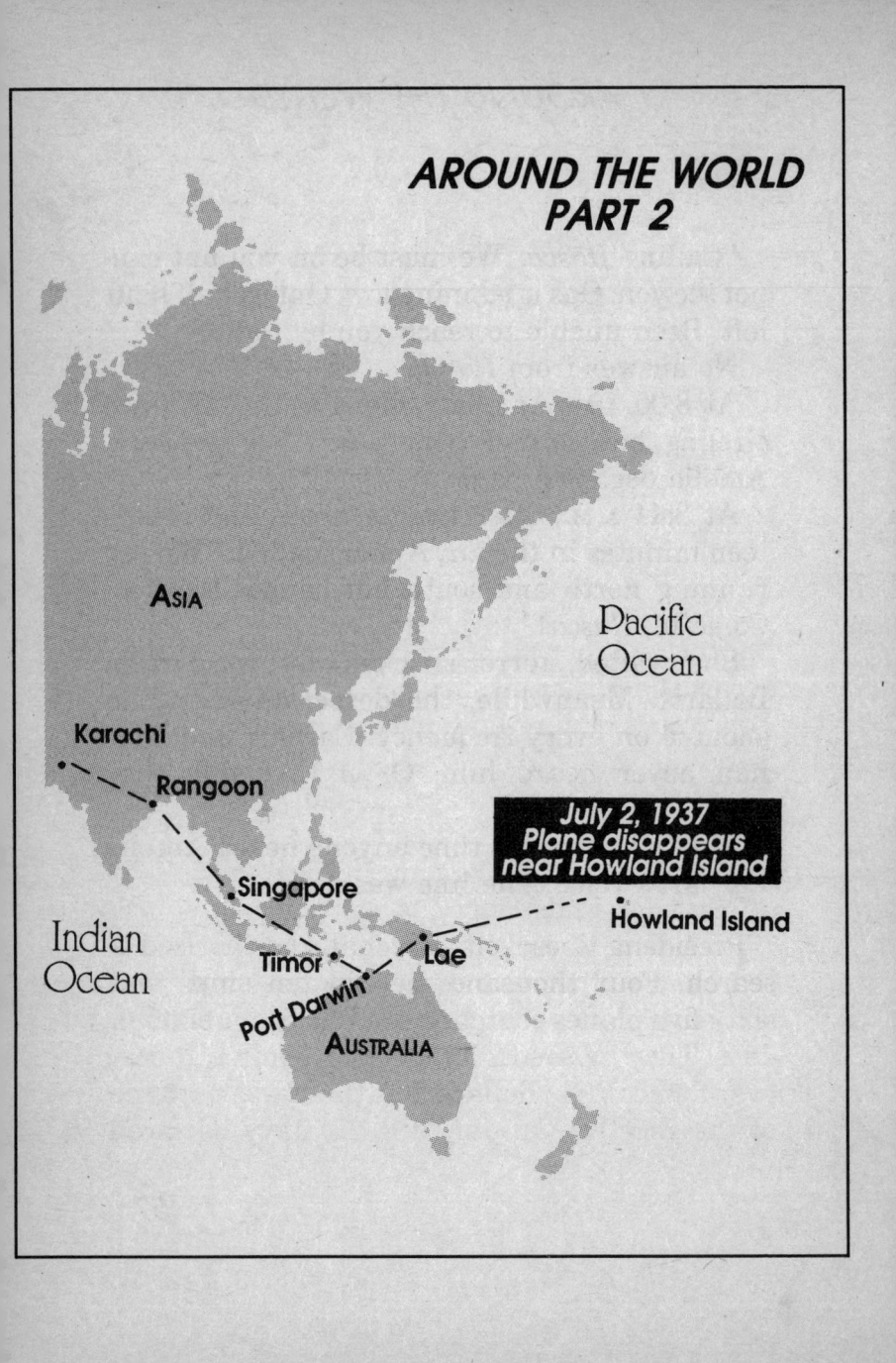

AROUND THE WORLD PART 2

Asia

Pacific Ocean

Karachi
Rangoon

Singapore

Indian Ocean

Timor
Port Darwin
Australia

Lae

Howland Island

**July 2, 1937
Plane disappears near Howland Island**

Chapter Six

Vanished!

The world was stunned by the news. Amelia Earhart and her plane had vanished! Headlines across the nation flashed the tragic story.

"Flyers Lost in Mid Pacific—Gasoline Supply Runs Low."

"Warship Catches Faint Signal."

"Amelia Floating in Pacific."

"Amelia Earhart Missing in Pacific."

"Disaster Ends Hope."

President Roosevelt personally authorized a search. Four thousand men in ten ships and sixty-five planes searched the Pacific for sixteen days. They covered 250,000 square miles. It cost over four million dollars. But there was no trace of the Electra. On July 19, the navy declared

WHAT HAPPENED TO AMELIA EARHART?

that the search was over. The world mourned the loss of Amelia. Everyone believed that she had lost her bearings and run out of fuel. Amelia Earhart had died at sea.

Meanwhile, tension was brewing in Europe and the Pacific. People's attention turned to other things. By 1941, the United States officially entered World War II. For a while, the legend of Amelia Earhart was forgotten. The war took the headlines now.

Then, in 1943, *Flight to Freedom* came out. It was a Hollywood movie about a famous woman pilot. She flew a secret mission across the Pacific. She got lost at sea on purpose. Then the U.S. Navy had an excuse to search Japanese-controlled islands. This was otherwise forbidden by the League of Nations.

The movie followed reality in one way. The Japanese did control several islands in the Pacific. But they were to be used for peaceful purposes only. Then, in 1937, the Japanese quit the League of Nations. The United States became suspicious. They thought the Japanese might be using the islands for military reasons.

An aerial photo of Howland Island, where Amelia and Fred were supposed to have landed. Note how narrow and small it is.   UPI/Bettmann Newsphotos

Many American servicemen saw the movie *Flight to Freedom* while they were stationed in the Pacific. They thought the story seemed true. And they thought the pilot in the movie was meant to be Amelia Earhart. Rumors began. Had Amelia really been on a secret mission when she disappeared?

In March of 1944, U.S. Navy Lieutenant Eugene Bogan was stationed on the Marshall Is-

WHAT HAPPENED TO AMELIA EARHART?

lands. They were formerly under Japanese control. They were also right near Howland. Bogan had a very interesting conversation with a native named Elieu Jibambam. Elieu said that a friend of his, Ajima, saw an American woman flier. Her plane had come down on a reef. The pilot was picked up, alive, by a Japanese ship.

Then, in September, there was an article about Amelia in the *American Weekly*. The U.S. Marines had captured Saipan. Saipan was one of the many Marianas Islands in the North Pacific Ocean. The article said that some marines found a photo album with pictures of Amelia in a captured barracks. But Amelia didn't take an album like that on her flight. Still, people thought the album held a clue to her disappearance.

George Putnam read the article in the *American Weekly*. He also heard the rumors. He wanted to know for certain what happened to his wife. He got permission to travel all over Saipan. He talked to many people. But he found no evidence of Amelia. Some people said he didn't want to find her because he had a new

VANISHED!

wife. But by the time he went to Saipan, he was already divorced.

George was convinced that Amelia had run out of fuel. He believed she died in an emergency landing. But he also thought that the U.S. search for Amelia achieved two things. One was to look for his wife. The other was to get information about Japanese-controlled islands. But he said Amelia was definitely not a spy.

George's visit to Saipan answered his questions about Amelia, but the rest of the world was still asking. In 1944 and 1945, U.S. Army Postal Corps Sergeant Thomas E. Devine was based on Saipan. He saw a twin-engine plane locked in a hangar at Aslito Airfield. He read the registration number. It was NR16020—the same number as Amelia's plane! Sergeant Devine wanted others to see the plane. But shortly afterward there was a fire and explosion in the hangar. The plane was destroyed. Sergeant Devine claimed that the U.S. Army got rid of the plane on purpose. What were they trying to hide?

About a year later, a native woman took Devine to a Japanese cemetery. She led him to a grass-covered spot. An interpreter spoke for her.

"Here lies a grave of two Americans. They were fliers. One was a woman." Was it Amelia?

When the war ended, the rumors kept on. The navy denied that Amelia was involved in military operations. But the many Americans in the Pacific kept talking to natives about Amelia.

A navy dentist on Saipan had an assistant named Josephine Blanco. She had another story about Amelia. In 1937, when Amelia disappeared, Josephine was eleven years old. She was bringing lunch to her Japanese brother-in-law. He was in a restricted area. Josephine had a pass to enter.

"Want to see some American fliers?" whispered her brother-in-law. He took her to see a woman dressed in pants and a shirt. Her clothes were unusual for a woman at that time. But they were just like Amelia's. The pilot's hair was cut short, like Amelia's. A male pilot was with her. The man was tall, like Fred. Japanese soldiers led the aviators into the woods. Josephine hid behind some bushes. She covered her ears when she heard the gunshots. The soldiers returned alone.

VANISHED!

Years later, Josephine married and settled in California. Her name was now Josephine Akiyama. In 1960 a CBS journalist in San Francisco read her story in a local paper. His name was Fred Goerner. He had become very interested in the Earhart mystery.

Fred Goerner went to Saipan four times and interviewed more than two hundred people. He really wanted to know what happened to Amelia. He spent five years investigating. He even checked the role of the U.S. military in Amelia's last flight.

Fred finally came to a conclusion. He believed that Amelia was on a spy mission! She had detoured to take photos of Japanese military sites, but she got lost in a storm and had to land at Mili Atoll in the southeastern Marshall Islands. She was about seven hundred miles northwest of Howland. A Japanese fishing boat rescued Amelia and Fred. The aviators were then taken to several islands. Finally they were brought to Saipan. There they were questioned and died. Fred Goerner did not know if they were executed or died in prison.

The Japanese prison on the island of Saipan where it is thought that Amelia may have been held prisoner and then died. UPI/Bettmann Newsphotos

Goerner wrote a book about his theory. It was called *The Search for Amelia.* In it was a photo of Amelia sitting on a car. The car had a Japanese driver. The caption said the photo had belonged to a Japanese officer. It was taken of Amelia while she was on Saipan. But later, the evidence changed. It was proven that the photo was actually taken before Amelia's flight. The

VANISHED!

driver in the picture worked for Standard Oil right in the United States.

The photo may have been false evidence, but what about the rest of Goerner's theory? It fit with previous rumors that Amelia was seen on Saipan. *Hundreds* of people claimed they saw Amelia on Saipan. Were they *all* mistaken?

Marines Everett Hansen and Billy Burks were on Saipan in 1944. Their superior officer, Captain Griswold, gave them an unusual order. He led the marines to a grave.

"Men, I want this grave excavated," he commanded. "Start digging." Hansen and Burks dug up the remains of two bodies. Captain Griswold took the remains away.

"That was sure a strange assignment," said Hansen.

"Yeah, it was," replied Burks. "I'm going to ask Griswold what that was all about."

"Hey, Captain," shouted Burks. "What's going on?"

Captain Griswold turned to the men. He grinned. Then he winked at them and said, "Did you ever hear about Amelia Earhart?"

WHAT HAPPENED TO AMELIA EARHART?

Was Griswold implying that the bodies were Amelia and Fred? Why did the army want them dug up? Or was Griswold just teasing Burks? If it was just a joke, then who were the two bodies?

Many people wanted to solve the Amelia Earhart mystery. They contacted her mother, Amy Earhart. What did she think happened to Amelia? In 1949 Mrs. Earhart told reporters that she thought Amelia had been on a government mission. "Amelia said there were things she couldn't tell me," Mrs. Earhart said.

But Amy Earhart was very old by 1949. Was it easier for her to believe that her daughter had been on a noble mission? Was it too painful to think she had just lost her way and died at sea?

Still, there was too much evidence to be ignored. It seemed that Amelia had been seen on Saipan and the Marshall Islands. But the stories contradicted each other. Some natives said they saw the Electra crash. Others claim the plane landed intact. Some say they saw wrecked remains of the plane. Still others saw the U.S. Army destroy it.

And what of Amelia? There are stories claim-

VANISHED!

ing Amelia was killed immediately. Other witnesses say she was jailed. A few say she lived in a hotel and could travel in a restricted area. Most say she died of dysentery.

Many islanders were shown photos of Amelia. "Was this the woman?" they were asked. The answer was always "Yes."

Was it possible that Amelia Earhart was still alive?

The plane that was to have taken Amelia Earhart round the globe. The Bettmann Archive

Chapter Seven
What Happened to Amelia Earhart?

One researcher was sure Amelia still lived. He was Joe Gervais. Gervais agreed with Fred Goerner that Amelia was a spy. Gervais said Amelia was supposed to fly over the Marshall Islands and take photos. Then she "got lost" on purpose. Gervais tried to visit Saipan to investigate. But he was not a reporter like Goerner. He couldn't get permission to go to Saipan. So he went to Guam instead. There he talked to people who used to live on Saipan. He looked into the case for six years.

In 1965 his research took a surprising turn. Gervais was eating lunch in a restaurant on Long Island in New York. He gazed out at the

WHAT HAPPENED TO AMELIA EARHART?

Long Island Sound. The lapping of the water on the rocks made him dreamy. He glanced to his left. There he saw something very interesting. It was an emblem on the sleeve of an elderly woman's blouse. He had to speak to her.

"Excuse me, madam. I see you're wearing an oak-leaf decoration. Isn't that only worn by holders of the American Distinguished Flying Cross?" Meanwhile, Joe was thinking, "She looks just like Amelia Earhart would have looked at sixty-eight years old. I'll keep talking to this woman."

"I used to be a pilot," the woman said.

"My name is Joe Gervais. I'm very interested in the history of flying. Won't you join me for some coffee? We can chat awhile."

"I'm Irene Bolam." They shook hands and sat down. She told him she was also a member of the Ninety-Nines and Zonta.

Amelia had belonged to those associations also! The Ninety-Nines was an organization of women pilots. Amelia had been one of its founders. She was one of ninety-nine original members. But certainly Irene Bolam could be one of the other ninety-eight. Zonta was a professional

WHAT HAPPENED TO AMELIA EARHART?

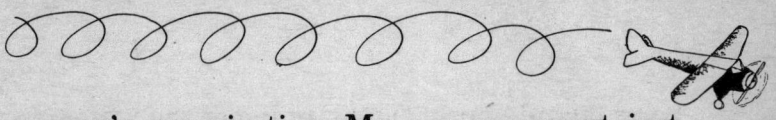

women's organization. Many women, not just pilots, belonged.

Still, Joe became convinced that Irene Bolam was really Amelia. She was married to a man named Guy Bolam. Gervais believed that the name Guy Bolam was a code name. Each letter stood for a letter in the name of an island in the Phoenix Group. He read the underlined letters vertically.

>   GARDNER
>   ENDERBURY
>   SYDNEY
>   BIRNIE
>   PHOENIX
>   HULL
>   CANTON
>   MCKEAN

Then he assigned each letter a number. He came up with the numbers 172,13,4, and 21, and compared them to numbers on a map: 172 degrees and 13 minutes west longitude; 4 degrees and 21 minutes south latitude. He had a very detailed map of the Pacific. These numbers were the

WHAT HAPPENED TO AMELIA EARHART?

exact location of a lagoon on the northwest shore of Hull Island. It was the same lagoon where a U.S. seaplane had landed to look for Amelia.

Did Joe Gervais discover a hidden code? Many people thought his theory was crazy. He just wanted to find an answer to the mystery. Other names could be made from letters in the island names, also. Few people believed in his code.

But Gervais firmly believed Amelia had finished her spy mission. He claimed that President Roosevelt didn't want to admit that he had used Amelia as a spy. The world loved Amelia. Roosevelt would have been unpopular for risking her life.

Had Amelia secretly returned to the United States? Did she take a new identity to keep the government's secret and her own privacy? Was her new name Irene Bolam?

Gervais investigated further. He checked on the deed of Irene Bolam's house. It was actually owned by Floyd Odlum. Floyd was Jackie Cochran's husband, and Jackie was Amelia's best friend. In fact, Jackie headed an organization of women ferry pilots during the war. In Jackie's

WHAT HAPPENED TO AMELIA EARHART?

autobiography, she claims that she found files on Amelia in Tokyo. The files were in the Dai-Ichi Building, the general headquarters for the Japanese Imperial Air Force. Jackie didn't write about the contents of the files. No one else has seen them. Why would the Japanese military have files on Amelia? What happened to the papers?

Jackie Cochran also claimed to be telepathic. She was *sure* that Amelia died at sea. But was she covering up for her best friend?

Gervais also found photos of a Lockheed Electra with the same serial number as Amelia's plane. It had crashed in the California mountains. Gervais decided that Amelia had purposely crashed her plane in Hawaii on her first attempt to fly around the world. The world believed that her Electra was taken away for repairs. Gervais said that the plane was actually switched for another, more powerful one. He claimed that Amelia had flown a larger military plane to perform her spy mission, and the original Electra was flown by another pilot at some other time. That pilot's job was to dispose of the original plane. And there it sat, hidden among

WHAT HAPPENED TO AMELIA EARHART?

the trees of a remote mountain forest in California.

Paul Mantz, Amelia's old aviation buddy, told the press that he had a "sister" plane to Amelia's. It was a Lockheed Electra also. He had gotten permission to use Amelia's serial number on it. It was *his* plane in the photograph. But Paul was also a good friend of Amelia's. Was he helping her keep the secret?

Irene Bolam didn't like Joe Gervais's research. She said his theory was a big mistake. She threatened to sue him if he didn't leave her alone. She said she had been a friend of Amelia's—nothing more. Gervais met another woman pilot named Viola Gentry who claimed she had known both Amelia and Irene. Viola Gentry told Gervais that in 1937 Irene Bolam was Irene Craigmile before she married. Gervais got a copy of Irene Craigmile's pilot's license. It was issued on June 1, 1937. That was the same day Amelia took off from Miami on her flight around the world.

Irene Craigmile never picked up her license. Was Irene Craigmile a made-up name? Did someone pretend to apply for a license for her?

WHAT HAPPENED TO AMELIA EARHART?

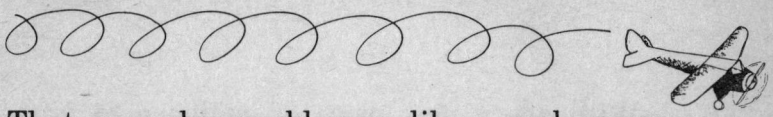

That way, she would seem like a real person. Someone might discover Amelia pretending to be Irene. The pilot's license for Irene could be a fake "proof" that there really was an Irene Craigmile Bolam.

Irene Bolam refused to supply a birth certificate or fingerprints. Why wouldn't she give absolute proof that she was not Amelia Earhart? Was Gervais so annoying that she just wanted to be rid of him?

Joe Gervais had a meeting with Amelia's and Irene's friend, Viola Gentry. He told Viola that there were a lot of people interested in the Earhart case.

"It could be worth a lot of money to find out what really happened on July 2, 1937," he commented.

"That's what Amelia says," answered Viola.

"You just said, 'Amelia *says*,' like she's alive!" said Joe.

"I did?" replied Viola. "I meant to say Muriel, Amelia's sister. I often confuse their names," she explained.

Was Viola telling the truth? Or was she covering up a careless slip of the tongue?

WHAT HAPPENED TO AMELIA EARHART?

With every new piece of evidence to prove that Amelia had survived came information to disprove it. It was very confusing. No one knew what to believe. Whenever the mystery of Amelia Earhart came to rest, something stirred it up again. Many people thought she *had* survived. The government and friends of Amelia's were quick to claim that she had died at sea. They had reasons why the new evidence was false. But wouldn't they be the ones to cover up the true story if they were in on the spy mission? Many people thought so. Others said she surely ran out of gas and met a watery grave on the bottom of the Pacific.

The U.S. government has released many documents from 1937. There is no evidence in them that Amelia was involved in a secret operation. But since 1937, we have seen many other secret government operations like Watergate and the Iran-Contra affair exposed. Does the U.S. government have other secrets we have not learned about?

The Roosevelts denied that Amelia had been on a mission. Arthur Schlesinger, a historian and expert on the Roosevelt administration,

WHAT HAPPENED TO AMELIA EARHART?

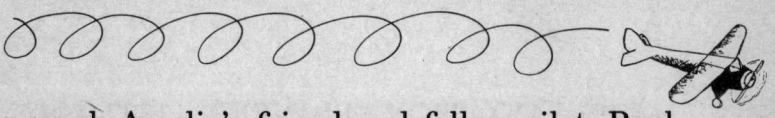

agreed. Amelia's friend and fellow pilot, Paul Mantz, believed she died at sea. Psychic friend Jackie Cochran says the Lockheed Electra landed at sea, floated for two days, and sank. Lockheed aeronautical engineer Kelly Johnson said Amelia couldn't have been spying. The only camera she had was a Brownie. And she'd been airborne for twenty-three hours. "So help me," he said, "that's all the time they had fuel for." She must have died at sea.

The Japanese government said they never saw Amelia. Japanese historian Masataka Chihaya said that the tales of finding the aviators were false. Were they denying the truth that Amelia and Fred were executed on Saipan? The world would have been very angry if the Japanese had harmed Amelia.

The mystery of Amelia Earhart may never be laid to rest. Somewhere in the world, there may be something or someone waiting to be uncovered that will tell us what REALLY happened. Will some underwater diver find the remains of her plane on the ocean floor? Or will someone, someday, find a hidden grave right here in the United States: HERE LIES AMELIA EAR-

WHAT HAPPENED TO AMELIA EARHART?

HART, AVIATION PIONEER, 1897–*1997*? Maybe she's sitting by the window of her secluded country home this very minute. She's quietly sipping a cup of coffee that she holds in her wrinkled, bony hand. She's gazing out the window at blossoming flowers. On the mantel beside her rest her soft leather helmet and her goggles.

Will we ever know for sure?

WHAT DO *YOU* THINK HAPPENED TO AMELIA EARHART?

Bibliography

Children's Books

Nonfiction

Blau, Melinda E. *Whatever Happened to Amelia Earhart?* Milwahkee, Wisconsin: Raintree, 1977.

Parlini, John. *Amelia Earhart: Pioneer in the Sky.* Champaign, Illinois: Garrard Publishing, 1962.

Sloate, Susan. *Amelia Earhart: Challenging the Skies.* New York: Fawcett-Columbine, 1990.

Fiction

Howe, Jane Moore. *Amelia Earhart, Kansas Girl.* New York: Bobbs-Merrill, 1961.

WHAT HAPPENED TO AMELIA EARHART?

Adult Books

Nonfiction

Backus, Jean L. *Letters from Amelia 1901–1937.* Boston, Massachusetts: Beacon Press, 1982. Letters to Amelia Earhart's mother.

Goerner, Fred. *The Search for Amelia Earhart.* New York: Doubleday, 1966.

Klaas, Joe. *Amelia Earhart Lives: A Trip Through Intrigue to Find America's First Lady of Mystery.* New York: McGraw-Hill, 1970.

Loomis, Vincent V. and Jeffrey L. Ethell. *Amelia Earhart, the Final Story.* New York: Random House, 1985.

Lovell, Mary S. *The Sound of Wings: The Life of Amelia Earhart.* New York: St. Martin's Press, 1989.

BIBLIOGRAPHY

Putnam, George Palmer. *The Last Flight.* Fort Lauderdale, Florida: Orion Books, 1988. Actual dispatches. letters and diary entries from Amelia Earhart's final flight.

Rich, Doris L. *Amelia Earhart, a Biography.* Washington, D.C.: The Smithsonian Institution, 1989.

CAMELOT WORLD
A FRESH LOOK AT OUR WORLD

THE MYSTERIOUS CAT   76038-X/$2.95 US/$3.50 Can
by Elizabeth Garrick

HOT MACHINES by Gregory Pope   76039-8/$2.95 US/$3.50 Can

SECRETS OF THE SAMURAI   76040-1/$2.95 US/$3.50 Can
by Carol Gaskin

A KID'S GUIDE TO HOW TO SAVE THE PLANET
by Billy Goodman   76041-X/$2.95 US/$3.50 Can

GREAT DISASTERS by David Keller   76043-6/$2.95 US/$3.50 Can

DOLLS by Vivian Werner   76044-4/$2.95 US/$3.50 Can

UFOS AND ALIENS   76045-2/$2.95 US/$3.50 Can
by William R. Alschuler

A KID'S GUIDE TO HOW TO SAVE THE ANIMALS
by Billy Goodman   76651-5/$3.50 US/$4.25 Can

SECRETS OF THE DOLPHINS   76046-0/$2.95 US/$3.50 Can
by Diana Reiss

WHAT IS WAR? WHAT IS PEACE?   76704-X/$2.95 US/$3.50 Can
by Richard Rabinowitz

A KID'S GUIDE TO HOW TO STOP THE VIOLENCE
by Ruth Harris Terrell   76652-3/$2.99 US/$3.50 Can

Buy these books at your local bookstore or use this coupon for ordering:

Mail to: Avon Books, Dept BP, Box 767, Rte 2, Dresden, TN 38225   B
Please send me the book(s) I have checked above.
☐ My check or money order—no cash or CODs please—for $_____ is enclosed (please add $1.50 to cover postage and handling for each book ordered—Canadian residents add 7% GST).
☐ Charge my VISA/MC Acct#_____ Exp Date _____
Phone No _____ Minimum credit card order is $6.00 (please add postage and handling charge of $2.00 plus 50 cents per title after the first two books to a maximum of six dollars—Canadian residents add 7% GST). For faster service, call 1-800-762-0779. Residents of Tennessee, please call 1-800-633-1607. Prices and numbers are subject to change without notice. Please allow six to eight weeks for delivery.

Name_____

Address _____

City _____ State/Zip _____

CMW 0892